A HOUSE FOR LITTLE RED

Modern Curriculum Press
BEGINNING
TO
READ
Series

A House for Little Red

Margaret Hillert

illustrated by
Kelly Oechsli

ER
HIV
11/08

Library of Congress Catalog Card Number: 79-85953

ISBN 0-8136-5513-7 (paperback)
ISBN 0-8136-5013-5 (hardbound)

18 19 20   11 10 09 08

Here, Red.
Here, Red.
Come here, Little Red.

Come here to me, Little Red.
Run, run, run.
Here is a cookie for you.

8

I want to play.

We can run and jump.

One, two, three.

Here we go.

Here is something.
Here is a blue ball.
Jump up, Little Red.
Jump up, jump up.

10

Go, Red, go.

Go and find the ball.

Oh look, Red.

Look here.

Here is something for a house.

I can make a house for you.

Go in, Red.

Go into the house.

Oh, oh.

It is not a house.

You look funny.

Here is a yellow house.

Go in here.

Go in, go in.

Oh my, oh my.
The house is down.
It is not for you.

Come, Little Red.
Come and look.
We can find a house.

17

Here is a little house.
I see something in it.
One, two, three little ones.
It is not for you, Red.

18

Look up, look up.

I see a house up here.

Oh, my.

It is not for you.

Look here, Red.

Look down here.

Here is a little house.

See the mother.

You can not go in here.

20

Come, Red.

Come away.

It is not for you.

Oh, here is Father.

Father is big.

Father can help.

Father, Father.

Can you make a house?

Can you make a house for Little Red?

I can. I can.

Come and see.

I can work.

You can help me.

E

Down, Red, down.
You can not work.
You can not help.
Go away.

Oh, Father.
The house is big.
Where is Red?
Come, Red.
Go into the house.

Red is in the house.

A big house.

A blue house.

A house for Little Red.

Margaret Hillert, author of several books in the MCP Beginning-To-Read Series, is a writer, poet, and teacher.

A House for Little Red

A boy finds a house for his dog with his father's help, told in 49 pre-primer words.

Word List

7	here		and		into
	red		jump	14	it
	come		one (s)		not
	little		two		funny
8	to		three	15	yellow
	me		go	16	my
	run	10	something		down
	is		blue	18	see
	a		ball	20	mother
	cookie		up	21	away
	for	11	find	22	father
	you		the		big
9	I	12	oh	24	work
	want		look		help
	play		house	27	where
	we		make		
	can	13	in		

30